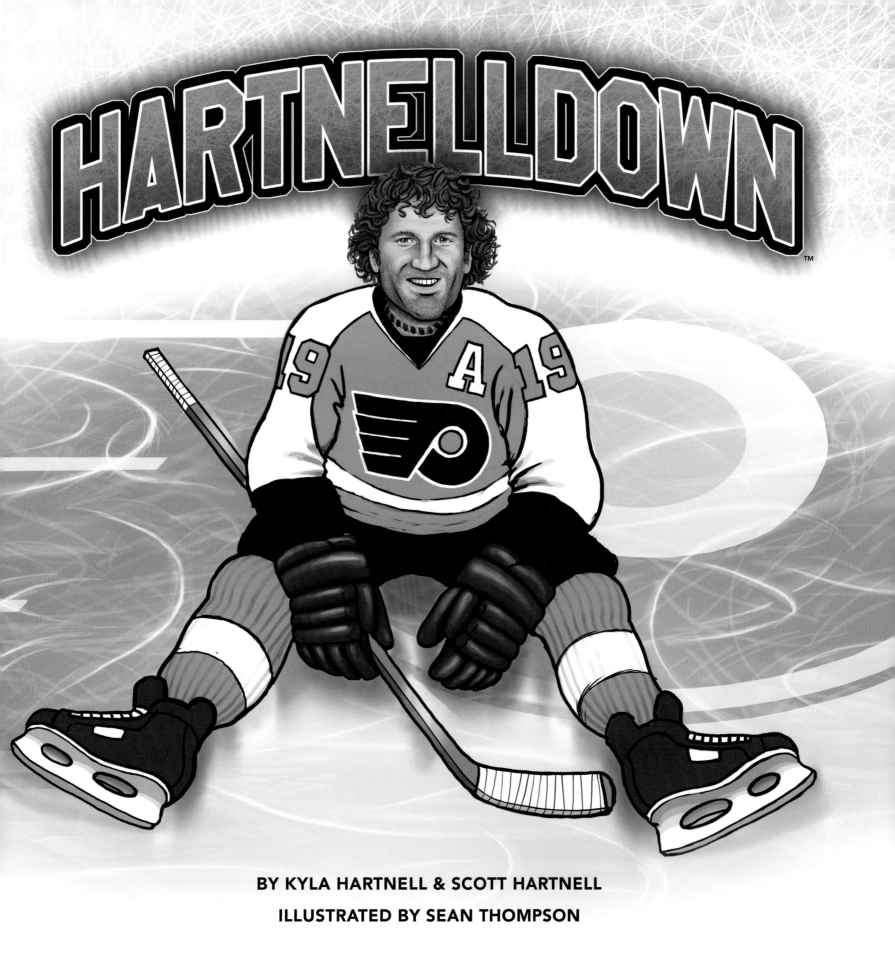

HARTNELLDOWN ™

BY KYLA HARTNELL & SCOTT HARTNELL

ILLUSTRATED BY SEAN THOMPSON

Published in the United States by hartnelldown foundation

www.hartnelldown.com

Authors: Kyla Hartnell & Scott Hartnell

Illustrated by: Sean Thompson

Publisher: hartnelldown foundation

Project managers: Bill Hartnell & Carrie Wood-Grillo

Book design and layout: Dean Pickup

Printed in Canada by Friesens

2013/1
First Edition (Hard Cover)
ISBN 978-0-615-91806-8

WELCOME TO #hartnelldown™

The #hartnelldown foundation was created in 2012 to help both kids and adults become physically active and healthy. Hockey is a big part of my life, and I want to give back to the game and to the communities that have supported me throughout my life and career. I am overwhelmed and grateful for the support we have received.

#hartnelldown fans rock!
#BOOM

– SCOTT HARTNELL, FOUNDER

When I was two I learned to skate
My sister, she could skate real great,

But I would slip upon the ice

hartnelldown... not so nice!

So up I got and grabbed a stick
Lots of practice would do the trick,

My mom, she helped us all to skate
My brothers, they could skate just great,

My coach was great (he was my dad)
He showed me all the tricks he had,

We had a rink in our backyard
So I could learn to shoot real hard,

But when I swung my stick like this

hartnelldown... and I missed!

But never did I want to quit
Not even when I learned to hit,

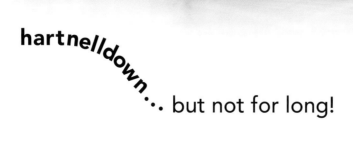

The other teams were big and strong

hartnelldown... but not for long!

Run the track and hit the gym
Stretch and abs and then a swim,

Draft day came and I was wary
The NHL seemed kind of scary,

SCOTT HARTNELL

From Eston Mite to the Big Show

hartnelldown... now I'm a pro!!!

When dressed in orange I have no fear
I love to wear the Flyers gear,

Don't touch my long and curly locks

hartnelldown... and in the box!

The corners are where I belong
Control the puck, be big and strong,

My coach tells me to set a screen
So D–man's shot can't be seen,

Tip the puck, woo hoo, no sweat

hartnelldown... puck's in the net!

Deke the goalie, not once but twice
Slide the puck along the ice,

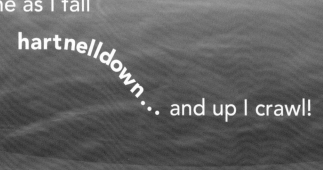

Past the goal line as I fall

hartnelldown... and up I crawl!

"Go top shelf," I tell the rookies

"Where Mama always keeps the cookies,"

Unless you want to go 5–hole

hartnelldown... and on a roll!

Odd man rush, I pick up speed
Tie game now, we need a lead,

Everyone just stops and stares
Puck hits my head and goes upstairs

But no! I'm tough and bound to win
I'll find a way and wear a grin,